Attack of the Giant Mutant Zombie Snail

Written by John Parsons
Illustrated by Ian Forss

Contents

1 Prologue 4
2 *Helix aspersa* 7
3 Escape! 18
4 Fugitive Snails 29
5 A Giant Mutant! 38

Meet the Characters

Aunt Augusta

A gastropod scientist.

Simon

Aunt Augusta's nephew.

Mum

Simon's mother and Augusta's sister.

Dad

Simon's father.

Amelia

Simon's sister.

A Giant Mutant Zombie Snail

One of Aunt Augusta's experiments.

Dear Reader

I was watching an old horror movie from the 1960s about a mutant alien monster that was terrorising a city, when I had the idea for this book. I wondered what would happen if a common garden creature suddenly became an enormous house-eating monster! Sometimes, science experiments have unexpected results!

John Parsons
Author

Our Backyard

1. The house
2. A giant mutant zombie snail
3. The vegetable garden
4. The back fence

1 Prologue

One of the downsides of living in a wooden house is that once a ten-metre mutant zombie snail gets a taste for timber, there's very little that stands between you and a ravenous mountain of grey slime.

I used to think my Aunt Augusta, who at this minute is hiding under the bed in the spare room, was a clever scientist. When she initially came up with the idea of genetically modified, chromosomally recombined gastropods that would only eat weeds, it sounded good in theory. But after six months of experimentation, certain practical shortcomings became apparent.

One of them was hungrily chewing its way through the living room wall right now!

On the plus side, there are no more weeds in our garden which, in fact, looks fabulous, resplendent even, with excellent crops of healthy cabbage, broccoli and other vegetables. But even Aunt Augusta, if she ever comes out from her hiding place, would have to admit the splintered, slime-covered house in the midst of our yard looks less attractive.

If you haven't read about this latest scientific advance, you might not be familiar with ten-metre mutant zombie snails. So let me enlighten you about their background. That way, you won't be totally surprised if you wake up one morning without a bedroom wall.

2 Helix aspersa

Aunt Augusta had long dreamed of working at the South Queensland University Institute for Research into Molluscs, or SQUIRM as it was fondly known by snail experts around the world.

She'd devoted her life to studying the common garden snail, *Helix aspersa*, so when she secured a six-month research grant from SQUIRM to investigate ways of genetically modifying it to transform it into less of a pest in gardens, she leapt at the chance.

Actually, she rolled around on her stomach, which was a gastropod scientist kind of behaviour. They celebrated good news in ways that only other snail scientists could really appreciate.

At the time, she was living in tropical North Queensland, because they have really humungous garden snails up there – so she packed her bags, headed south to Brisbane and came to stay in our spare room.

Mum, Dad, my sister Amelia and I listened to her snail tales, sometimes enthralled for at least a minute. At first, I'd just assumed that snails were somewhat boring. But after hearing Aunt Augusta regale us with stories of snails racing along at top speeds of 47 metres per hour, her adventures finding nests of snails under doorsteps, and the challenges of heliciculture (or snail farming), I realised they were really quite interesting. Compared to snail scientists.

"Has Aunt Augusta ever had a hobby?" I asked Mum one evening.

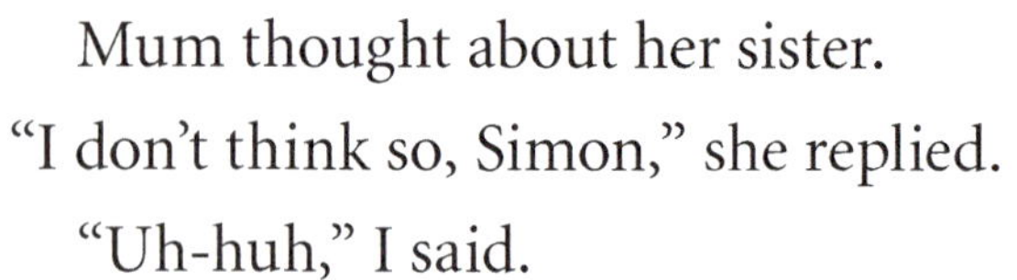

Mum thought about her sister. "I don't think so, Simon," she replied.

"Uh-huh," I said.

As a gesture of appreciation for being allowed to sleep in the spare room, Aunt Augusta offered to cook once a week.

"I don't do sausages and mashed potatoes, though," she warned us. "I only do French, Greek and Italian cuisine."

That sounded good in theory, until we'd eaten *beignets d'escargot* the first week, *kohli bourbouristi* the second, and *lumache alla romana* the third. Snail fritters, popping fried snails, and snails in tomato sauce.

"You must be getting busy at SQUIRM," said Dad, gingerly picking a crunchy piece of snail shell off his tongue. "It's a little unfair of us to expect you to work all day, then come

home and prepare us dinner. Why don't I take over your cooking night?"

"We are getting to a thoroughly exciting stage of research," admitted Aunt Augusta.

"That's settled then," Dad said, with a faint look of relief on his face. Mum, Amelia and I could have kissed him, then and there.

"What exactly are you researching, Augusta?" asked Mum, demurely dabbing tomato sauce from the corners of her lips.

"We're modifying the growth genes of *Helix aspersa*," she replied with a grin. "They're closely related to appetite. Our ultimate goal is to develop a genetically modified strain of garden snail that has absolutely no appetite for cabbages, broccoli or any other useful vegetables – but that does have

a voracious appetite for those plants we'd consider weeds."

"A snail that only eats weeds," said Dad. "Every gardener's dream."

"Exactly," said Aunt Augusta, beaming. "And if we can make it grow bigger at the same time, maybe even as large as a chicken, imagine the potential food benefits!"

"Snail roasts, with stuffing, gravy and plenty of cabbage and broccoli for Sunday dinners," I murmured to Amelia. "Now that's a brighter future to look forward to."

One of my chores each weekend was washing the family car. Dad always parked the car in a shady spot underneath a tree in our driveway which, in the southern Queensland sunshine, meant that when we all piled into the car, it was never hotter than 70 degrees Celsius. This, as Aunt Augusta helpfully pointed out, meant that our blood would not actually boil, but we would still be able to fry eggs on the dashboard in the eventuality of a power cut. Unfortunately, parking under a tree also meant the car was regularly frosted with bird droppings from the sparrows with highly efficient digestive systems that lived above. And that's why, every Saturday morning, I was issued with a bucket and squeegee and given five dollars to go and clean the car.

This particular week, the sparrows had obviously been eating a diet of concrete and PVA glue. I'd spent about five minutes slopping soapy water over the roof of the car when I noticed Aunt Augusta. She had her laptop under one arm and was placing strange, high-tech objects festooned with wires and aerials around the garden with her other arm.

"What are you doing, Aunt Augusta?" I asked.

"These are solar-powered, radio-controlled, gastropod-capture-and-retention devices, Simon," explained Aunt Augusta excitedly. "They charge up during the day, using photovoltaic cells on their upper surface. Then at night, when a snail enters the device, it passes over this sensor pad, a tiny residual current passes through its slime, and there's a resultant short circuit."

An onlooker might have thought I was fully focused on scrubbing a particular nasty green and white smear across the car's roof, but as far as Aunt Augusta was concerned, I was, of course, all ears.

"When the short circuit occurs, the electromagnet in this trapdoor is turned off and the door swings shut. When that happens, two tiny wires come into contact, completing another circuit, and a microchip sends a high-frequency radio signal through this antenna to my laptop, which is programmed to respond with an audible signal," she said. "Here, check it out!"

She unclipped the trapdoor of one of the devices and closed it. Her laptop burst into life with a tinny electronic rendition of "She'll Be Coming Round the Mountain" played on a kazoo.

"So it's a snail trap," I said.

"In layperson's terms," agreed Aunt Augusta. "I need to collect a fresh test population of *Helix aspersa* for the next stage of our experiment."

I had a great idea, one that would mean my car-washing days were over. I was pretty sure I could outrun a snail fleeing at 47 metres per hour.

"You know, for five dollars per snail, I could help you," I said.

"Really, Simon?" said Aunt Augusta. "That would be great."

3 Escape!

That was three months ago. Aunt Augusta happily purred over her new collection of fifteen garden snails, expertly captured from the wild, while I happily counted my new collection of fifteen five-dollar notes, expertly captured from her purse. It was a classic win–win situation. She didn't need to know I'd merely picked the snails off the bottom of the laundry step.

Three months later, however, Mum was not happy.

"But they need 24-hour supervision," protested Aunt Augusta, patting the roof of the suitcase-sized container she'd proudly brought home from the SQUIRM laboratory.

SQUIRM
LABORATORY

"Augusta," Mum said in a tone that Amelia and I immediately recognised as one of imminent danger. "Look at the size of them. They're as big as grapefruits."

"Yes, isn't it wonderful," said Aunt Augusta gleefully. "It's taken us three months, but we've successfully recalibrated their genetic code. A snail's DNA contains over 350 million genetic combinations, and we managed to find the exact pair we needed. Give or take ten thousand either way."

"And I can think of 350 million reasons why I don't want grapefruit-sized snails creeping around my spare room," said Mum.

“Really?” said Aunt Augusta in genuine awe. “That’s incredible, sis. Most brains only have about ten billion nerve cells, so thinking of 350 million things at once is pretty spectacular.”

Mum took a deep breath. “What if they escape?” she said, doing her best to remain calm.

“No problem,” replied Aunt Augusta airily. She pointed at me. “We’ve got the Crocodile Dundee of snail hunting sitting right over there. I don’t know how he does it, but that boy has a real talent for tracking and capturing snails in the wild.”

I pressed my nose deep into my textbook. I hadn’t told Mum about the

75 dollars yet, but thankfully, she was more concerned with Aunt Augusta's house guests at the moment.

"Alright," she said in an exasperated voice. "As long as you can categorically guarantee that they will not escape from that container, you can keep them in the spare room."

Aunt Augusta solemnly guaranteed, categorically, that they would not. And for an entire afternoon, and most of the night, she was true to her word.

"AARGH!" screamed Dad. "AARGH!"

Amelia and I rushed to the bathroom, where Dad was taking his morning shower, and banged on the door.

"Dad, are you OK?" called Amelia.

"AARGH!" replied Dad. We heard the water go off and an ashen-faced Dad unlocked the bathroom door. He was dripping wet, with a bath towel around his waist, and, with a trembling finger, he was pointing at the ceiling of the bathroom, above the shower cubicle.

A grapefruit-sized *Helix aspersa* hung calmly from the ceiling, two eyestalks the size of milkshake straws slowly waving in the steamy air.

"Right," said Mum, who had flung on her dressing gown and come to see what all the commotion was. "That's it." She stomped off down the hall towards the spare room.

"AARGH!" came another scream. "AARGH!"

Amelia and I raced down the hall, closely followed by Dad and his flapping bath towel.

Aunt Augusta was sitting up in bed, rubbing her eyes sleepily.

"What's up, sis?" she yawned.

"AARGH!" screamed Mum again.

The flimsy lid of Aunt Augusta's escape-proof container had been pushed off during the night and silvery slime trails wound their way across the wall. Pairs of waving eyes on giant stalks examined us from every corner of the spare room.

"AARGH!" screamed Mum, in case we hadn't heard her the first three times.

"Don't panic!" yelled Aunt Augusta, leaping out of bed. "Don't panic!"

"What if they attack us?" yelped Dad. "That one in the bathroom was peering at me very aggressively. I'm certain their giant snail brains are sizing us up at this very moment."

"Nonsense," said Aunt Augusta reassuringly. "We may have increased

their body size, but their brains haven't changed at all. They're miniscule. About one ten-thousandth the size of ours."

"Big mutant snails with miniscule brains," I breathed in astonishment. "Wow! They're like mutant zombie snails!"

Eventually, Mum and Dad calmed down, while Amelia, Aunt Augusta and I prised mutant zombie snails off the walls and ceiling of the spare room.

"Don't forget the one in the bathroom," said Aunt Augusta. Amelia headed down the hallway.

"There we go," said Amelia, when she returned, cradling a brown and white ball in her hands. "That wasn't so bad." She counted the snails, safely back in their container. "Thirteen grapefruit-sized mutant zombie snails."

I looked at Aunt Augusta and she looked at me. I knew we were both thinking the same thing.

Uh-oh.

4 Fugitive Snails

Try as we might, we couldn't track down the two missing snails. Aunt Augusta had wisely decided against telling Mum that there were still two unaccounted-for escapees on the loose, and I wasn't about to spill the beans about collecting fifteen of them for five bucks apiece.

Under Mum's watchful glare, Aunt Augusta loaded her container of recaptured runaways into the boot of our car. Dad was under strict instructions to drive them both to the SQUIRM laboratory and to not return until the snails, or Aunt Augusta, or preferably both, were safely locked up inside.

“Simon,” whispered Aunt Augusta, as she headed for the passenger door. “I’m relying on you to use your finely honed gastropod-stalking skills to track down that pair of snails. Shouldn’t be a problem for a hunter of your experience.”

I nodded confidently. How hard could it be? “Sure thing, Aunt Augusta,” I said. I scratched my head and frowned. “But these aren’t just wild garden snails. They’re mutant zombie snails.” I sighed and shook my head. “Couldn’t do them for under ten dollars each, I’m afraid.”

Two weeks later, I knew I'd grossly underestimated my hunter's fee. I'd searched the house from top to bottom, I'd searched the garden, and I'd even searched the bush in the reserve at the back of our house. The snails were nowhere to be found. They were experts in stealth. But I knew they were around somewhere.

I knew because, to my amazement and to Aunt Augusta's delight, the vegetable garden out the back was rapidly transformed into a completely weed-free environment. Not a dandelion, not a dock leaf, not a thistle remained. Free from competition, the cabbages, broccoli and other vegetables thrived. They'd grown so fast they were ready to harvest.

"Still no luck?" whispered Aunt Augusta over dinner one night. Another fortnight had passed, and I was rapidly tiring of having to eat steamed cabbage and broccoli every night. Aunt Augusta was desperate to recapture her snails to see how they'd coped on a month-long weeds-only diet, and I was desperate to let the weeds and the common garden snails back into the vegetable garden, to stifle and consume as many vegetables as possible.

I shook my head glumly. I was even starting to feel strangely wistful for a nice plate of *beignets d'escargot*.

"We may need to go back to good old-fashioned methods," she said. "I'll bring home some of my specially enlarged, solar-powered, radio-controlled gastropod-capture-and-retention devices."

"Give me one more night," I replied. "There's one thing I haven't tried."

Once everyone else had gone to bed, I crept out of my room. I must have been a curious sight, sitting in my pyjamas and dressing gown, shining a torch over the pristine vegetable patch. But, like generations of hunters before me, I was focused on outsmarting my prey. If they weren't going to snooze under a convenient rock or concrete step, I'd get them another way. There was too much at stake: 20 dollars or the possibility of another six months of cabbage with every meal. It was a stark

choice. And soon, my exceptional talent for tracking and capturing snails in the wild was rewarded. Like four marbles on flexible springs, I saw the eyes of two unmistakably mutant zombie snails appear from the undergrowth beyond our yard.

"My babies!" cooed Aunt Augusta, after I'd tiptoed into the spare room with the two giant snails. She was sitting up in bed, stroking the slimy snails affectionately. "Ouch!" she said suddenly, drawing her hand back. "What was that?"

"What was what?" I said.

Aunt Augusta ran her hands over the snails once more. "Go and turn the light on, Simon," she muttered. I flicked on the switch and returned to sit on Aunt Augusta's bed.

Aunt Augusta examined her snails closely. "Hmm," she said. "Love darts."

"What?" I asked, puzzled.

"When snails are about to reproduce, they fire tiny calcium darts into each other," explained Aunt Augusta. "They help stimulate hormone production. They're called 'love darts'." She pointed to a small, glistening fragment embedded in the side of one of the snails. "About two weeks later, they lay eggs."

I looked at Aunt Augusta and she looked at me. For the second time in a month, I knew we were both thinking the same thing.

They'd been out for two weeks. Uh-oh.

5 A Giant Mutant!

There was good news and bad news.

The good news was that, unlike normal garden snails, only one egg had been laid instead of eighty. The bad news was that, when it finally hatched from its location hidden deeply beneath the soil of the reserve behind our house, it was ten metres long and six metres high.

The smaller eucalyptus trees in the reserve were the first to go. The giant mutant zombie snail crushed them in its path and hungrily devoured them – leaves, branches, trunks and all.

Aunt Augusta and I had been sitting out on the back porch, watching the sun set, and we watched aghast as the mountain of grey slime headed towards us in the twilight.

"Oops," said Aunt Augusta. "Looks like we might have slipped up with one of those ten thousand genetic combinations either side of the appetite gene."

The giant mutant zombie snail pushed its way through the back fence and started on Mum's prized camellia trees.

"But they're supposed to eat weeds," I hissed at Aunt Augusta. "Why is it eating trees?"

Aunt Augusta looked sheepish. "Technically, I only programmed them to avoid cabbage, broccoli and other common garden vegetables," she said. "Normally, that would mean they'd only be able to eat small garden weeds." A camellia tree disappeared under a

slab of ravenous grey gastropod. "I can solemnly and categorically guarantee I never expected them to grow that big," she said.

"AARGH!"

"AARGH!"

"AARGH!"

Mum, Dad and Amelia had come out to see what all the crashing, thrashing and rasping noises were. The muscles of the giant mutant zombie snail began pulsating and it started thundering towards us a lot faster than 47 metres per hour, taking a wide arc through the back yard to avoid the cabbages and broccoli.

"Everybody inside!" yelled Mum.

"Don't panic!" recommended Aunt Augusta helpfully.

Mum ran into the living room and picked up the phone, dialling the emergency services number as quickly as she could.

"What seems to be the problem, ma'am?" came the calm voice at the other end.

"We're being attacked by a ten-metre long giant mutant zombie snail," said Mum, gasping for breath.

"Well, be sure to let us know how that turns out for you," said the voice sarcastically. The line went dead and Mum looked at Dad in astonishment. Suddenly, the last of the sunset was obliterated, as a giant slimy blob of grey slapped itself against the window, and a gnawing, rasping sound filled the entire house.

"Timber weatherboards," breathed Aunt Augusta in admiration. "It even likes timber weatherboards."

"It's chewing through our house?" yelled Dad in disbelief.

"No, no," smiled Aunt Augusta reassuringly. "Snails don't have teeth. They can't chew."

"Then what's that noise?" demanded Mum.

"It's just a radula. It's like a rough, raspy file that snails use to grind up their food."

I don't know about anyone else, but that made me feel a lot better. Our house wasn't going to be chewed to bits, it was going to be pulverised into slimy sawdust instead.

"Augusta!" snapped Mum. "This is all your fault. How are we supposed to get rid of that ... that thing out there?"

"Oh, that's easy," replied Aunt Augusta. "Are there any vegetables in the fridge?" she asked meekly.

So anyway, here we all are, hiding under our beds, surrounded by as much cabbage and broccoli as we could find in the vegetable cooler to ward off a giant mutant zombie snail.

"Don't panic!" I can hear Aunt Augusta calling from underneath her bed in the spare room. "Everything will be fine."

I can hear her dialling a number on her mobile phone.

"Hello," she says. "Is that Professor Blagdon from the Southern Polytechnic's Laboratory for Avian Technology? I've got a great idea for SPLAT: a genetically modified, chromosomally recombined sparrow that only eats giant snails. Interested?"

Giant mutant zombie sparrows. That sounds good in theory. But, like Aunt Augusta's current scheme for genetically modified, chromosomally recombined garden creatures, I don't think it will end well. If you've ever had to wash the family car, and scrub bird poop off the roof, you'll know why.

Evidently it's been a while since Professor Blagdon washed his own car.

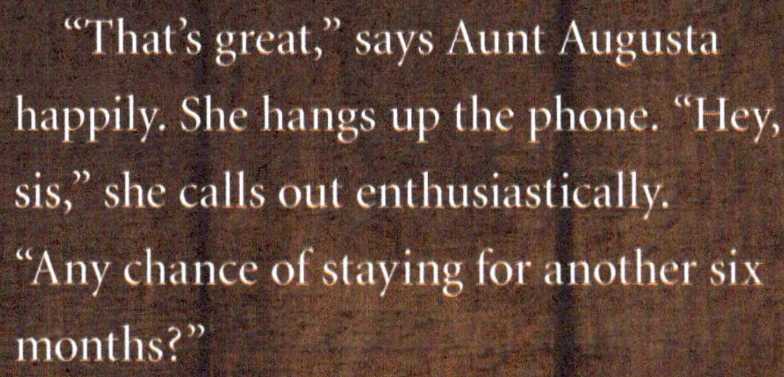

"That's great," says Aunt Augusta happily. She hangs up the phone. "Hey, sis," she calls out enthusiastically. "Any chance of staying for another six months?"

"AARGH!" comes Mum's reply. "AAAAARGH!"